CAUSTIC

A Novel

TAMESHA EDWARDS

© 2018 Tamesha Edwards
All rights reserved.

ISBN: 1985167271
ISBN 13: 9781985167278
Library of Congress Control Number: 2018902160
LCCN Imprint Name: Tamesha Sherish Edwards, San Leandro, California

To My Readers

God gave me a dream in 2002. I struggled with how to interpret my dream into words. With his blessing, the title *Caustic* was developed, and the character of Margaret was created.

Margaret's life is beyond tumultuous. I enjoyed developing each character and writing this story; I hope you'll become engulfed in the story line and love the story as much as I loved writing it.

I am appreciative and thankful for your support; have a wonderful read.

—Tamesha Edwards
Website: https://tameshaedwards.com

ACKNOWLEDGMENTS

My beautiful bears, Tykeria Rattler and Elijah Daniels, Mommy loves you dearly.

To my family members—my mother, Joann Ned; my father, David Edwards; my twin sister, Ariel Edwards; my niece, Amaya Thomas; my nephew, Devin Curtis; my grandmother Madie Richard; and my aunt Jrusha Grant—I love you all.

Thank you too, my dear friends Natasha Andrew, Robert Daniels, Leonard Garcia, and Astrid Howard.

Special thanks for moral support to Heidi Cherry, Daisy Johnson, and Janie Ward.

INTRODUCTION

When one's soul is inflamed, there's a need to try to decipher a constant nightmare. Some individuals are unable to ungrasp the violent spirits that have attached to their souls.

There is a constant burning from the inner torment of inflicted wounds that may or may not help one overcome the caustic torment of one's mind, spirit, and soul that causes one's eyes to be blurred with blood. This is what Margaret has become.

CHAPTER 1

It was unbeknown to me that I would end up in a medically induced coma before my twenty-fifth birthday. Let's start at the beginning. It was 2002, and I was at home in my apartment.

I primped myself and sat on an old maple chair, wondering if the mirror would shatter to pieces. Slowly, I brushed my hair with one stroke after another. I wondered if I even began to measure up to every little girl's fairy-tale dreams of true beauty. On the contrary, my fairy tale of true beauty involved words that I would never fully comprehend, probably due to never being called beautiful. I didn't wear a sash that read Beauty Queen, but as pathetic as it may seem, this was what had become of me. I was told day after day that I was a pathetic piece of trash. Being beautiful was something that wasn't relatable to me.

Trash was disposable and unable to coexist in a home of torrid hostility; it was something I couldn't fathom. We are worn out from wanting to see the world as this place of what we human beings call "beauty" every day of our lives. That was not realistic for me and didn't correlate to my thought process. What is beauty? If you can't see it, that's a rhetorical question. Then the questions of why, where, what, who, when, and how formed in my mind. I constantly harped on this idealistic meaning, but I couldn't see or find the beauty in the woman I was becoming.

It was Wednesday. I finished getting dressed, tidied the loft, and headed to the farmers' market, walking the city streets. I smelled the authentic scents of poultry, fruit, vegetables, oils, soaps, and candles that vendors were selling; my eyes were wide open, and I wanted a cup of straight-black coffee. I could hear the street musicians jamming a mile away as if it were Miles Davis playing for me. I visualized myself sashaying through the green meadows, but I was walking the streets in the middle of December on a misty day. Suddenly, I felt palpitations.

I couldn't believe what my eyes were witnessing. I had to be hallucinating. But it wasn't a hallucination. There he was in his brown woolen suit, my father, beaming with that crooked smirk of his and walking hand in hand with his brand-new <u>family</u>. The woman looked quite timid, as if she were one of those docile women who had no control of her marriage. She was younger than I expected; she looked as if she was in her early twenties, and the little doll baby was a young girl of around five or six. She had two braided pigtails with blue-and-white ribbons hanging down to her shoulders and a lollipop inside her mouth. I watched the little doll baby twirl her dress around with the innocence of a child just enjoying herself.

It was picture-perfect; it reminded me of those old Kodak pictures that my mother used to take of me with that white-and-black camera. Instantly, there was a flash that would snap anyone out of daydreaming, and then you had a picture of yourself. It seemed as if my picture had been taken; the flash had captured my soul for a few seconds, and just like a statue, I was unable to move. My heart beat fast, the palms of my hands were sweaty, and beads of sweat were running down my head. I felt like I was hyperventilating.

Anxiety had crept in, and a heart spasm fluctuated between my shoulder blade and my heart. This was one of those silent killers of moments that everyone has. I became silent but had a conversation with myself and reiterated, "Snap out of it. Get a grip. Walk; walk fast, faster, and faster. Don't run; do not draw attention to yourself."

I just made it to the front entrance of the boutique on the left. "Excuse me, miss, can I try on that dress in the window?"

"Yes, you can."

"Where is your dressing room?"

"Toward the back entrance on the right. Excuse me—what's your dress size?"

"I'm a size six."

"It will take a few minutes; I must check our stock room to see if we have your size available."

"Okay, no worries." Entering the dressing room, I checked to see if there was a lock. I leaned against the mirror in the dressing room, closed my eyes, and began to drift back to my childhood.

I could vividly see and hear my momma saying to me, "Oh, Margaret, you look so pretty, like a woman in that pink-and-white dress. Go show your daddy."

"Look, Daddy! Momma said I look like a little woman."

"Go to your room!" shouted my daddy. Then he started to yell at me. "Stop prancing around this house like a cheap whore! You won't wear no dress like that ever in this house. Do you hear me? Do you hear me?"

I ran upstairs to my room, burying my head in the pillow, crying heavily, and sobbing. I just wanted to go hide underneath my covers after hearing my dad yelling at me. I could hear voices from downstairs; my momma was talking to my dad. "Douglas, you did not have to be so cruel!"

Next, my dad screamed, "What, woman?"

Then my momma spoke calmly to my dad. "What's going on with you, Douglas? You used to be so happy with us; now you're just afraid of everything. As a matter of fact, I'm tired of your madness."

I tiptoed out of my room to the top of the staircase, peeping over the banister. There was my dad standing up and looking directly in Momma's face, saying to her, "Don't you ever, woman, try to talk down to me! I put food on this table and a roof over your head."

Momma's dismay was expressed on her face. She then said, "Douglas, don't you dare talk to me like I'm supposed to be grateful. For what? You keep me in this house like a prisoner of your love. There is no way can continue to stay in this marriage. I will take our daughter and go."

In my mind, I was saying to myself, "Go ahead, Momma; tell Dad that we are leaving. Good riddance. Let's just go bye-bye." But I knew that this was not going to go over well with my dad, and I wished Momma had just kept quiet.

Out of nowhere, Momma began to scream, "Keep your hands from me, Douglas!" Dad started slapping and dragging Momma by her hair and throwing her against the wall; I could hear her saying, "Oh, you show me how manly you are! You're a weak coward that gets off on beating on me!"

Then my dad started acting like he was Ike Turner. "You can't leave! Where you going to go? To your drunken mother? Your father? Wait a minute—what father? He got tired of you and your mother and ran out on the both of you. What you going to do? Without no education, you just another statistic."

Momma then said, "I'd rather be labeled a statistic than lay up in this house and pretend we have a good marriage when in fact it's been over for years. I'm done!"

Dad screamed at the top of his lungs, "Ungrateful bitch! Lousy worthless nothing of a woman! You remind me of my mother. She wasn't nothing either. After my dad made a home for her, she could not cut it!"

Momma kept feeding into his words, and then she said, "Douglas, this is what you see of me? Your wife, the mother of your child—being uneducated, lousy, and ungrateful? I am all this is in your mind? Well, like your mother, I'm leaving and taking my daughter with me. See, she left you with a man who hated women; it has been passed down to you. She's turning over in her grave, knowing the miserable bastard she carried in her womb enjoys entering his daughter's room at night and bedding his flesh and blood."

Dad was still screaming. "Ryanne, you think it's that easy? You just go walk out of here!"

Momma then said, "It's that easy. Touch me. The police will know everything you have done to our daughter. Margaret? Margaret, sweetie, get your coat and shoes, and come downstairs."

Then my dad looked toward me and said, "Get your little ass back up those stairs." Then it was as if his eyes turned red, and he morphed into this beastly looking man. I was staring at a demon, the same demon who would enter my bedroom at night and cover my mouth with his hand as he just took the life out of me, night after night. He said to my momma, "After everything I've done for you? I made you the woman you are. You're going to just leave?"

Momma replied, "Douglas, you're sick; you need help. You like little girls, not me." Turning her back, she headed up the stairs.

I suddenly witnessed my father grabbing the steel poker from the fireplace and strike the back of her head. Blood started to drip from her head. He grabbed her from behind, pulled her by the hair, and started to pull her down to the ground. He punched his fist into her face, kicking her in the stomach and pounding her head on the floor. My momma looked up at the staircase and hollered at me to go back to my bedroom. I couldn't move; I froze and became mute. I just couldn't help my momma.

I watched as he dragged her into their bedroom. He placed her on her stomach. Ripping her panties apart, he began to sodomize her. He penetrated her and then took his penis out of her butt. He forced himself to release again in her mouth. Her nose was filled with blood; she was gasping for air, and her body lay almost lifeless on the floor.

I couldn't hear what my dad said to my mother as he knelt beside her. My mother's eyes widened as my father whispered in her ear, "Our daughter's pink, fleshy, wet pussy tasted and felt better than your pussy ever felt. Now suffocate on your blood, bitch."

He then got up, walked over to the edge of the bed, and lit up a cigarette. I crawled on my knees to my mother and said, "Momma, Momma, oh, Momma, please, Momma, wake up! Don't leave me here." I held my momma in my arms, rocking her back and forth.

My dad said, "Stop sobbing, or I'll have you sob on my dick. Your momma is all right. Go back to your room."

"Father!"

"Get back upstairs; she's all right."

"Father, Momma is not breathing."

"What you want me to do, Margaret? Go get your momma a towel, soap, and a small bucket of water now. Wash her body, and help me put her gown on."

"What are you talking about, Dad?

"No, she's not dead. She is sleeping, and when the ambulance is called, you better go along with my reasoning for your mother's death. Do you fucking hear me? Or you'll be lying next to her. So she stops breathing. You know your mom is a junkie, that go on these frequent drugs binges, and sometimes, she exchanges sex with drug dealers to support her drug addiction. I've notice money missing from our bank account. This time one of the drug dealers beat your mom, because she tried to sell him fake jewelry. Now go to your room before you end up like her."

Staring out the window, I said, "God, please don't cast my soul into the pit of hell." All night, I wrestled with the fact that my mother was never coming into my room to kiss me on the forehead and that I would never smell the scent of rose petals, the fragrance that she sprayed onto her body. To whom would I talk when I felt alone?

A few days passed. Everyone believed exactly what my father had told the police—that my momma was a frequent drug user, that she would go on these binges for days, and that he had no knowledge of her whereabouts until she returned strung out or beaten up. It was strange how he seemed to portray this upright, dignified man who was the embodiment of what a husband and a father is supposed to look like. This man was a stone-cold murderer. This man took my momma's life in front of his own daughter's eyes.

Inside the funeral home, everyone was crying and mourning my momma's death. Sitting in the pew, I was disgusted with myself. Pastor Murdock preached my momma's service, and it was strange that he never, ever met my momma. I couldn't recall my momma ever being the church type. I paid attention to Pastor Murdock; I could hear him saying, "Well, well, well." I wondered why this pastor was saying "well" repeatedly. He needed to get to the point. It was as if he struggled with his words; he seemed quite tongue-tied. Here he went again with the word "well."

I thought, "Let me listen. This is the last time I'll be with my momma. The best thing to do is respect my mom's homecoming."

The pastor continued to preach. "Well, well, well. On this Wednesday morning, it wants to be no sad morning for Sister Ryanne Jones. You'll want to grieve Sister Jones's death. Ryanne gone up yonder, where you, you, you, you, and you trying to get to. She gone to be with God and his son, Jesus Christ. See, God chose her to leave this place we call earth. Her body lays in this casket, but her soul is in heaven. You don't hear me church. Amen! Amen!"

The people at the funeral yelled, "Yes, Pastor Murdock, go ahead! Preach, Pastor."

The pastor kept up his performance. "You all sleeping today! Are you alive today? Answer me, church! Are you sleeping, or are you alive?"

Everybody started jumping up and down. One lady started dancing up and down the aisle of the church. Even my father started his two-stepping, shouting, "Thank you, Preacher!"

I couldn't believe the blasphemy of my father in the house of the Lord. He was the spawn of devil. Why hadn't he been stricken down by lightning right here inside this church?

I thought, "Wait a minute. Why haven't most of the people been struck down? My momma hardly knew these people, and Aunt Clara, my father's sister, didn't even like my momma." I had always heard her ask my father what he was thinking of when he married my momma.

My momma was gorgeous to look at; she was what you called "dark and lovely." She had thick, curly, coarse brown hair that brushed against her cheeks every time she tried to put her hair into a ponytail. She was five feet seven, and her body was shaped like a Coca-Cola bottle. She had almond-shaped eyes that sparkled in the sunlight; in the moonlight, it was like looking at an oil painting. Her grace and poise just intimidated my aunt Clara, mainly because she looked more like my father's twin brother than his older sister. Aunt Clara did not have any kids, and my momma told me that she had a liking for women, whatever that was supposed to mean. I never quite understood why my momma did not just say that Aunt Clara was a lesbian with masculine features.

Now, Aunt Clara was up in front of the church, about to talk over an hour about nothing. All I could hear were all her lies that she insisted on telling inside God's house. What was wrong with my family? Were they all sick in the head? I thought, "Momma, I know you're here walking around, looking at all these people, and shaking your head. I can especially see you wanting to drag my father by the neck and cast him into the pit of hell where he belongs."

My father got up and walked over to say a few words about my momma; the murderer was going to really speak about my momma. This was so unbelievable. Where was the lightning bolt? Why wasn't he struck by lightning? I thought, "Please do not let me have to hear his voice speak untruth."

He said, "Good day, everyone. Thank you all for coming here today. This is not a day to be feeling somber. Rejoice that my wife, your sister in Christ, is gone to heaven to sing with the angels and to watch over all of us. She would not want you all to be crying. She would want to hear all of you laughing and praising God that she is gone home to her father in heaven, where you all are trying to make it to. It's as if yesterday, I was saying 'I do' to the most beautiful woman I have ever seen in my life. She was the mother of my daughter.

"She was a blessing to each one she encountered. This wonderful woman lies not in a wooden casket but a sixty-five-hundred-dollar brass casket with gold lining, nothing but the finest. I spared no expense; she's going out in style. No maggots or worms any of those creatures from the dirt will touch her. She will be resting in style, do you hear me, church? Although she lies in front of us, we will never see her again. I will truly miss my best friend"

I was in disbelief that he was informing every one of the money he spent on a casket. I remember my momma handling the family's life insurance, and she wrote everything about her burial service. I couldn't believe the load of bull that my father was saying.

He was sobbing and trying to make himself cry; to make matter worse, he was putting on the performance of a lifetime. I felt like standing up and saying, "Ladies and gentlemen, the Oscar goes to Mr. Douglas for the leading male role in portraying a grieving husband and father."

I felt that I should just get up and walk to the front of her casket and just let everyone know that I was an accessory to the murder. As I sat in the pew, I thought, "Momma, I'm so sorry. This is a theatrical mess. Father is acting like he is going to faint. Maybe he'll faint and crack open his head, and they'll bury him. Don't worry; I won't bury him in the same burial plot. Oh, my. I can't believe these thoughts are in my head at your funeral, Momma."

Pastor Murdock said, "We will now have a song from Sister Ryanne Jones's daughter, Margaret, singing 'Up Yonder.'"

I said, "I decided to sing another song I wrote for my momma. Please bear with me." And I sang.

> I love you. Oh, Momma, why did you have to go so soon?
> We just recently met; I recently just started to understand you.
> Oh, Momma, why did you have to go so soon?
> I love you and feel that you left me,
> Momma, here with no
>   directions, nowhere to turn.
> Oh, Momma, why did you have to leave me so soon?

The teaching had just begun, and now it's already gone. I try to
    understand why.
I know that you are no longer here. I can't be strong because
    we only know what really went on. So, Momma, you loved
    me.
Even if you never had the chance to tuck me in at night,
    to kiss me on my cheeks to say, "I'll see you in the morning
    sunlight."

The entire church was in tears. People were standing up, clapping, and coming over to hug me after everyone viewed the body. It felt so surreal; it was as if my mom was with me, holding my hands during the viewing of her body for the last time.

During the burial, everyone was tossing red roses in my momma's casket. I do not know what came over me. I began to scream, "Oh, Momma, oh, Momma, I can't let you leave me! Don't go, Momma." I held on to the casket as it was lowered into the ground.

I wanted to just be buried alive in the ground with my momma. I deserved to die a slow and painful death for being a coward and not telling the truth to the police about my momma's death. My aunt Silva, my father's baby sister—another sibling who did not attend the funeral—claimed that there was a terrible accident on the freeway and that she just couldn't make it in enough time. Aunt Silva should have been an actress; she was the only person I knew who could make my momma's funeral about herself. She was what people called a loose woman. My momma would always throw away the glasses and utensils that Aunt Silva would use. It got so bad that when she would come over, Momma went from cleaning the toilet with bleach and Ajax powder to replacing the toilet seat.

I asked my momma why she went through all this trouble, and she would just say, "Loose woman. Everybody wagging a tail; she is jumping on it." My aunt looked clean, but my momma always told me that looks are deceiving. Why was my aunt Silva wearing this gigantic red-lace hat with a veil? As a matter of fact, she was wearing red everything from head to toe. I couldn't believe she wore a red-lace thong; I could see it because the dress was stuck inside her butt cheeks. She had no bra on; my goodness, Momma was absolutely right: Aunt Silva was a loose woman.

My aunt Silva started to say, "Margaret, Margaret, Margaret. Come on, child; you will see your mother again in heaven. She would not want you to be acting in such a manner. She would want you to be strong and go on with your life. Stop this; stand up and wipe your tears. Your mother is at peace. She is no longer in pain. No longer will she have to suffer with that demon that she dealt with during her time on earth."

"Stop what, Aunt Silva? I can't let her go. Momma, please come back for me. I just want to go with my momma."

"Listen to me," said Aunt Silva. "Look directly into my eyes, Margaret. You must focus on what is happening right now and that your mother has gone to a better place. She is watching over you. God says in the book of Hebrews, 'Never will I leave you; never will I forsake you.' You keep that scripture with you and turn to God when you need his words and love."

I replied, "Thank you, Aunt Silva."

CHAPTER 2

I could hear the salesclerk from outside the dressing room say, "Excuse me, excuse me! Miss, are you okay in there?"

I started to think, "Oh my God, I can't believe that I'm unaware of the salesclerk calling out to me from outside the dressing-room door."

The salesclerk's voice intensified. "Miss, are you okay in there?"

Instantly, I said, "Oh, my! Yes, I'm okay."

She then proceeded to say, "I'm going to hang the two dresses on the door for you to try on. Please come to the counter if you want to purchase the dresses, or just leave the dresses on the hanger inside the dressing room."

I said, "Thank you." I exited the dressing room, walked over to the cashier's counter, and purchased the red dress. The salesclerk smiled and said, "Miss, you are going to rock this dress."

I smiled and said, "Thank you." Pushing the door handle open, I walked out of the boutique and headed home to my apartment. As entered my loft, I walked straight to the canopy bed. I started wondering why I was unable to find closure with my past and why I could not face my father. I knew there was a serious problem that was happening and that I needed to call my psychologist. That would be the best solution to my problem. Or should I basically resolve my problem by self-medicating? What was up with me?

I lay on my stomach and told myself to get it together. I turned onto my back, needing desperately to self-check back into reality. I was seeing that bastard who helped with my creation. All the turmoil that was embedded inside me was supposed to have been long gone from my memory. I got out of the bed, walked to the kitchen, and opened the refrigerator door. I grabbed a bottle of sparkling water and gulped one swallow after another. It was as if my brain had exploded with memories fading in and out. Was this all that was left—my painful memories? Oh God, I do not have one good memory that I can reflect on that related to my childhood.

Walking back to my room, I lay down on the bed. I was beginning to think about the death of my mom. Where was that little white bottle on my nightstand? I needed to go to sleep. Being restless for the rest of the night was not an option for me. I was suddenly too anxious; maybe a few of these little white pills would take the edge off. Slowly, I felt my eyelids become heavy. As I drifted off to sleep, the phone started to ring. I could barely see my telephone, but I heard a lady's voice saying, "Hello? Hello, Margaret? It's your aunt Silva. I'm downstairs; buzz me up."

I replied, "Huh, Aunt Silvia? Something is happening to me. I can barely hear you. My heart is beating fast."

As I gripped the telephone receiver inside my hands, my head began to feel faint. I was panting for air. The telephone slipped through my fingertips and fell to the ground. I started to have convulsions, foaming at the mouth, blood dripping from my nose. In my last breath of consciousness, I called out for my aunt Silva for help. I heard her screaming through the telephone, "Margaret, Margaret, can you hear me?"

Aunt Silva sounded frantic, and she started shouting, "Excuse me, sir! Can the apartment-maintenance man open this door? Call the police and an ambulance for apartment one oh three!"

The maintenance porter responded, "What's wrong, ma'am?"

Silva said, "Please help me! It's my niece Margaret." Aunt Silva ran up the stairs, gasping for air.

The firemen arrived before the ambulance and police. The firemen busted the door down, and one of the firemen said, "Ma'am, she's lying on the bedroom floor."

The paramedics arrived; as they assessed Margaret, they noticed bleeding from the side of her head. Then, not a minute later, the police walked into the apartment and started to inventory the areas. They found a bottle of pills spilled on her nightstand; they had caused an overdose. The paramedics took her vitals and noticed a weak pulse; they placed her on the gurney. Aunt Silva grabbed Margaret's purse and asked the paramedics, "Will my niece be okay?"

A paramedic responded, "We won't know until we get her to the hospital. Her eyes are open."

An officer said, "Hi, I'm Officer Brady. I'll follow the paramedics to the hospital to ask you a few questions."

Aunt Silva replied to the officer, "Why do you need to ask questions about my niece?"

Officer Brady replied, "Ma'am, these are regular, routine questions; I need a few minutes of your time."

Aunt Silva followed the paramedics into the ambulance. She was still frantic and unable think straight about what was happening to Margaret. Aunt Silva knew that she couldn't call anyone. She thought, "If she wakes up and sees her father or my sister, she'll likely go into shock and never talk to me again."

Arriving at the hospital, Margaret was rushed into an operating room. The clerk at the front desk handed a clipboard to Aunt Silva and asked her to fill out the medical-consent form and to write the medical-insurance information. Aunt Silva said, "I beg your pardon?"

The clerk then said, "Ma'am, we need for these medical forms to be completed and filled out in their entirety."

Aunt Silva told the clerk, "Just give me the paper work; I need to know what you all are doing to my niece."

The clerk told Aunt Silva to relax and reiterated, "Ma'am, our doctor will take excellent care of your niece. She's in good hands."

Then Officer Brady walked up to Aunt Silva, who said, "Excuse me, Officer, I'd like to offer my sincere apologies; I forgot your name."

The officer replied, "I am Officer Brady. If you have time for a few questions, would you like a cup of coffee?"

Aunt Silva said, "No, thank you. Thank you for asking."

Officer Brady began his interrogation. "Why do you think a young woman your niece's age would be taking pain medication?"

Aunt Silva replied, "I have no answer. My niece is a private person."

Officer Brady then went a step further and crossed the line with Aunt Silva. He said, "Is she suicidal?"

Aunt Silva started to frown and tried to control that temper of hers by saying in a calmly respectful voice with a little sass, "My niece is fighting for her life. All you can ask is whether she was trying to kill herself?"

Officer Brady tried to reassure Aunt Silva. "Ma'am, these are routine questions. I'm trying to understand what has happened to your niece."

Just as Aunt Silva was going to respond to Officer Brady, the doctor entered the waiting-room area. "Are you a family member of Ms. Jones?"

"Yes, she is my niece."

"My name is Dr. Hutchinson. Your niece has endured a traumatic brain injury—such as blunt trauma; sometimes patients are put in an induced coma. Shutting down functions can give the brain time to heal and permit surgery on the brain. There is a blood clot that I and the other surgeons do not want to remove surgically. The impact of the fall and the medication in her system are the reasons for her to be put in an induced coma. We will monitor her overnight. The other important thing about Margaret's condition is that she could become brain-dead and may not be able to come out of the coma. It would be a good time for you and your family to just be prepared, in case you might have to decide to take her off ventilation."

Aunt Silva said, "Excuse me, Doctor. At this very moment, I am not thinking about tomorrow; at this very moment, you do everything for my niece. Where is your chapel?"

"On the first floor, to the right of the elevator."

"Thank you, Doctor. I will return shortly."

Aunt Silva entered the chapel and knelt at the altar. "God, it's me praying for my niece. This child came into this world hurting; I never wanted to believe the words she spoke of my brother, her father. I'll trade places with her in a heartbeat. Please, Heavenly Father, have mercy on our child. She has endured so much; she needs you now more than ever."

Silva walked into the hospital room of her niece. She looked at her lifeless body and wondered why this was happening. She thought, "What caused my niece to want to take medication that she did not need to be taking?"

She held Margaret's hand inside her hand tightly. "Baby girl, you're going to pull through this. Don't give up on life; fight with all your strength."

The officer entered the room. "Excuse me, Ma'am?"

"Yes, Officer Brady?"

"My apologies to you for asking you questions earlier about your niece. No disrespect intended. I need to get an accurate account of what events led to your niece being hospitalized to write my report."

Aunt Silva said, "Officer Brady, I know that you're doing your job. Honestly, believe me—my niece had a bad reaction to her medication."

"I accidentally overheard you talking with God about you not believing your niece," said Officer Brady. "Madam, I will let you be. There is a need for me to be detailed in my report. I will check back in a few days and complete my interview with you and will keep your niece in my prayers that she has a speedy recovery."

I could hear my aunt's voice and an unfamiliar voice, one I hadn't heard before. I wanted to speak and open my eyes, but for some reason, my eyelids had become heavy. I couldn't speak, but I was alive. It was as if this nightmare that I had lived my entire life would continue to haunt me. There were words that I was unable to say. "Aunt Silva, you're unable to hear me; I'm lying lifeless in this bed. But whatever you do, fight for me since I'm unable to fight for myself."

"Excuse me, miss. My name is Keagan. I'm one of the nurses who'll be caring for your family member. I'm going to give her medication intravenously."

I thought, "Oh, please do not let this woman give me any medication that is not going to wake me up but prolong my condition to remain in a coma."

"Go ahead and care for my niece." As usual, my aunt would do what was needed for me to get well. The medication was beginning to kick in to my system; calmness was coming over my entire body. I could feel myself drifting back to my teenage years.

CHAPTER 3

I was haunted by my thought process and unable to wake up from the nightmare of reliving the past. The year when I was in twelfth grade was the most difficult year of my life. A year had passed since the death of my mother. Vividly, as if it had been yesterday, I remembered arriving home from my friend's house. I had enjoyed myself at the high-school dance I'd attended the night before. I was unaware that my father had found out about the dance. I cheerfully returned home full of life, not suspecting that my father was going to go into a rage and that this unexpected event would take my life in an entirely new direction.

    Entering the house, I walked by my father and ran up the stairs, not knowing that he was behind me. My father opened the door and told me to take off my underwear.

"What?"

My father started to grab me by the hair. "Margaret, you have been a nasty little girl. Give me your panties. Take them off right now!"

"Please don't, Daddy!"

"Tell me what you did!" Out of nowhere, I felt the back of his hand across my mouth. He was yelling, "Look at you! Nasty little whore! I saw you with that boy, all up on him!" He was enraged and out of control.

I was totally frightened, not knowing what was about to happen to me.

"Is this how you've been raised, Margaret? To be a Jezebel?" His eyes were wide, and his voice sounded off. "You've been a very bad, bad girl. Now, I must punish you, something I hate doing to you."

"Daddy, Daddy, I'll be good! I promise."

"I'm your father. Only whores say 'daddy.' Come here, Margaret."

"No!"

"You speak such filth to your father!" He grabbed my hair and pulled me down to the hardwood floor that needed to be gutted and replaced. I could feel the splinters inside my knees and toes. I was his rag doll. He dragged me to the bathroom, ripping every bit of clothing off my body. He started to turn on the hot water, watching the steam from the tub and the water filling up to the rim of the tub. I was forced to get into the tub; I refused to get inside willingly.

He bent the back of my neck, making me kneel. He threw me into the tub. He took the bristled sponge that he used to clean the grout from the floor tiles and began to scrub my entire body. I felt my face tingling and just wanted to die.

He was screaming, "Smell yourself! You reek with filth; you'll be clean from head to toe." The scalding-hot water was burning my body.

I said a silent prayer. "Please, Lord, let this be over. Please, Father in heaven."

He slapped and punched me as he dragged me into my bedroom. I tried to shout out, "No, I won't let you do this to me anymore!"

He continuously hit me, and as I fell to the ground with my father, we both began to wrestle with one another.

I kept hearing him say, "I'll do whatever I please."

As we wrestled back and forth, I thought, "This time, the outcome will be different." I reached my arms toward the dresser and instantly grabbed the scissors. With a strong grip, I closed my eyes, exhaled, and started to stab my father until he collapsed to the ground. I started to scream, "You can't do what you want with me this time!"

I ran downstairs and fell to my knees with the scissors in my hand. I heard a knock at the front door. I was unable to even reach for the doorknob; my aunt opened the door with her key to find me kneeling on the ground with a pair of bloody scissors in my hand. Frantic, my aunt asked me, "Where is your father?"

I did not respond. She searched the entire house to find her brother collapsed in a puddle of his own blood. She screamed for me to call for help, but she received no answer. She then called the police.

"Oh my God, pick up! Please, someone pick up the telephone!" She got the 911 operator.

"Hello, what is the nature of your call?"

She screamed, "Help me! Help me!"

"Ma'am, calm down. Let me assist you."

She was screaming through the phone at the operator, unable to fully explain what was happening.

"Ma'am, I want you to slow down. Relax yourself. What is the problem?"

"My brother has been stabbed."

"Check to see if you can feel vital signs."

"What do you mean, vital signs?"

"Ma'am, check his pulse and respiration. Can you tell me where he has been stabbed?"

"I can't tell."

"What position did you find him in?"

"He has collapsed in his own blood."

"Where do you live?"

"The address is 2231 Rosalind Circle. A white-and-green house. The cross street is Chester, and a silver Range Rover is parked in the driveway."

"I am giving dispatch this information, and the police and paramedics are nearby. Someone will be there shortly to help you."

"Thank you for your help."

"Ma'am, you're quite welcome. Do not hang up. Listen to me carefully. Do not move him. Go get a towel or a clean sheet, and apply pressure to any open wounds that are visible. Is there anyone else in the house who is hurt?"

"My niece is here. She doesn't seem to be hurt. A few bruises are noticeable. She's in a state of shock. I hear the police and paramedics. I am up here! Please come quick! Operator, I want to thank you for helping me."

"No need to thank me. I am doing my job."

"Hi, ma'am. My name is Lieutenant Smith; I will be the lead investigator handling this case. Please remain seated, ma'am, as I go and review my notes with the other officers."

He walked over to the rest of the officers inspecting the house and grounds. Lieutenant Smith gathered his information and walked over to Margaret sitting on the couch. She was not crying or saying a word. "Hi, is your name Margaret?"

She did not speak; she just vaguely looked at the lieutenant. "Margaret, did you see anyone? Do you know who would want to harm you and your father?"

As the paramedics carried my father downstairs on the gurney and hooked to oxygen, out of nowhere, I began to laugh out loud uncontrollably. I noticed that my father wasn't dead; my laughter and lack of concern had startled the police. The lieutenant asked me, "What seems to be amusing?"

My response was, "I couldn't even kill him; I could not even get that right."

Aunt Silva started to scream at me. "What's wrong with you, Margaret? You know better than saying something as awful as that about your father."

"Oh, Aunt Silva. Yes, I did; I meant every word of it!"

"Ms. Jones, I am going to have to take your niece to the police station for questioning."

"What? You will do no such thing! Margaret is coming home with me until my brother has recovered and we can get back to our normal lives."

The lieutenant could not believe his ears. "Ma'am, did you not just hear what your niece admitted to doing to her father?"

"Yes, I heard, but this child does not fully understand what she is saying. I need to call our family attorney."

"Unfortunately, I am not going to book her for attempted murder. I am going to talk with her. If she has not committed a crime, she will not need an attorney."

"I need to speak with my niece. Margaret, Lieutenant Smith would like for you to ride with him to the police station. I will be down there as soon as I see after your father."

I could give two cents about my aunt Silva seeing after my father. As I rode inside the back seat of the police car, I really wasn't worried if I ended up in juvenile. I needed to feel safe—away from a man who constantly bedded me whenever he chose to.

It was strange; the police station should frighten a young teenager like me. The sense of protection put me at ease with everything that was unfolding. I realized that this would likely not be on television—not because I'm African American but because my father happens to be a retired marine and the former chief of police for the city that I live in. Everyone loved him; politically, he was what every Caucasian or African American politician needed in his or her corner or pocket to help win campaigns.

My father had committed a heinous crime against his own flesh and blood. The black and blue would protect and serve their own before a mere civilian like myself. I was protected in a different way because as my momma had always told me, "You belong to God; he got you each and every day of your life."

I sat in the cold interrogation room; a social worker entered and started to talk at me instead of with me. It was as if I had already been convicted of attempted murder without any jury present to even hear my case. There was no one to talk with. Apparently, I was by myself, and no one would help me, the victim of molestation. And guess what? The molester was my father.

Two officers then entered the room, and I already knew that it was going to be a long investigation. Should I play this game of who did it or who didn't have clue, or should I tell the truth? No matter what, my father was going to come out of this smelling like a red rose blooming on a nice, sunny day. I would be hated because I defended myself from this narcissistic psychopath who would continue to look like a saint; I would be the child who attempted to destroy their town-hero image.

Life as I knew it was cruel, and the people surrounding me were supposed to be the ones who had pledged to protect and serve. However, they were the opposite and were a part of the nonsense that continued to perpetuate the judicial system. I could hear my aunt Silva and the social worker talk with one another as if I was not even in the room. The stare of disbelief from my aunt was what consumed me. Truthfully, my aunt was one person whom I loved openheartedly, but she would never take the place of my deceased mother. She was, however, the only person who I thought loved me as if she had carried me for nine months.

"Margaret, this kind lady has advised me that you need to be sent to a residential home that will help you with the grief of your mother and the other problems that have occurred since the passing of your mother."

"Aunt Silva, an institution is where they're going to send me."

"No, it's a reputable residential home for young ladies," Aunt Silva said.

"What about me finishing my senior year and going to college?"

"You will be able to complete your education at the residential facility, Margaret," the social worker said.

"I am having a conversation with my aunt; I do not think I addressed you in this conversation."

"Excuse my niece; she's normally not this mouthy."

"I want to go. If they're not charging me, then I am free to go home with you."

"Margaret, I love you as if you were my own child. You need help, and I am unable to give you the help you need. I want the best for you, my child."

"Aunt Silva, you want the best for me, so sending me off to some place you don't even know about is what you're telling me. Do not hug me; you're no better. You all are trying to keep me quiet, as if I'm at fault, to go away quietly."

Aunt Silva said, "Margaret, no one is against you. We only are concerned for the betterment of your welfare."

As I bent toward my aunt Silva's ear, I whispered, "Keep telling yourself that so you can sleep easy at night."

CHAPTER 4

Exactly one month had passed since I'd entered the Crane Mental Institution. Being told when to wake up, go to bed, take my medications, eat dinner, and bathe drove me insane. I got dressed and walked down the corridor to meet with the psychologist, Dr. Dunbar, who started off by asking me, "How you are doing? Have any new changes occurred since the last time we spoke?"

I stared blankly at the Dr. Dunbar.

"Margaret, you're not up to communicating today."

I looked at the doctor with a grim look.

"Listen and understand, Margaret, that I'm here for you to help you." He walked over and placed his hands on my shoulders. I tensed up at the touch of his hands. He removed them from my shoulder, noticing that I'd become somewhat uncomfortable.

Dr. Dunbar said, "Margaret, please accept my apologies."

I responded, "What are you apologizing for?"

Dr. Dunbar said, "I noticed that you became uneasy with me placing my hands on your shoulder. Would you like to talk about what made you feel this way?"

I said, "You have all my information in that manila folder that's on your lap. What do you want me to say? I'm tired of you and this place. It's as if I'm made to remain in a place where you only see me as what you read in a report."

Dr. Dunbar then replied, "This is your folder. Honestly, for myself, I never have believed everything I've read. Let me hear your side of this ordeal that you have been faced with. Explain to me why you're so angry. Help can be provided to you for your traumatic experience."

"Oh, Doc! You're like every other quack in this place. You're trying to examine my reaction by watching me from every angle. It's impossible to understand me; all quacks are the same."

"Margaret, I've been called worse names in my lifetime. Even though I've never been called a quack before, that's not going to stop me from trying to ask what's going on inside of your mind. What's with this defensive barrier? You've built up a wall to block out the inner noise you're suffering within."

I replied, "Come again?"

Dr. Dunbar said, "What is this tough-girl act?"

There was a knock on the door, and it was Suzie. "Your ten o'clock has arrived."

Perplexed, he then looked at me and said, "We'll resume this conversation next week at the same time, Margaret. I'm pleased to know that there's progress being made."

I replied, "Yeah, if you say so, Doc." Returning to my room, I looked outside the window, reminiscing about my happiness when my momma had been alive. I could vividly see my momma opening the door; I was walking through the dining room. Out of nowhere, my family and friends were wishing me a happy birthday, and I was blowing out the candles, making a wish that never came true. The opposite happened; I was forever in this agonizing pain of my mother death.

A tear began to fall down my cheek. "Hey, Mar!" Damn, I'd had enough of daydreaming. My roommate entered the room and informed me that we had a group meeting to attend shortly. "It's time for group; you know you don't want to be late. Mar, do you hear me?"

"Oh, yeah, I'll be there in a minute."

"Come on. Look, it's only an hour."

"Okay! Hold your horses."

"Are you all right? What's with the tears?"

"Don't mind me. Sometimes, I'm just happy. Sonja, now you know people cry when they're happy, and that happens to be me. Let's go."

Walking into group, I was always called out by one of the members in a confrontational manner. The discussion became heated and sometimes violent, as we were face-to-face with some low and high controversial communications with one another. I sat down next to Sonja, not even feeling the girls blatantly staring at me.

"Hi, and welcome to today's group discussion."

In unison, everyone responded, "Hi, how are you, Mrs. Bac?"

"Very well. So who would like to start off today's discussion?"

No one answered or volunteered to go first.

Mrs. Bac, asked Sonja to tell the group something about herself.

Sonja said, "You all call me church girl, because I carry a bible. Truth be told, my story wasn't written in the bible; it happen in this wicked world that we live in.

My judgers are those ladies, with the big hats, designer dresses and shoes, wearing red lipstick on their lips, praying the good old reverend make them his first lady. Little do them no, the reverend love fucking on little girls like me. All I got left is my bible."

Mrs. Bac, instantly called on Carmen to speak.

Carmen said, "Mrs. Bac, as of lately, I'm feeling like a punching bag. Taking blows to the chin, gut, chest and back. Enough is enough, flipping this bullshit to my advantage. Smooth knock-out, an upper cut to the head. Maybe then muthafuckas will get some common sense, and leave me the fuck alone."

Mrs. Bac, looked directly at me, and before she could even call my name.

I said, "Sharing my life story with the group, is something that I am not ready to do at this very moment."

Maxine, as usual, raised her hand.

"Okay, Maxine, you'll be the first participant."

Maxine said, "I'm doing so well. My kids are coming to see me for very first time since being admitted."

Mrs. Bac replied, "That's really good news."

Now, the only problem with this situation is that Maxine is only seventeen and has no kids. The abuse afflicted on Maxine is something she couldn't even begin to rationalize. She loved her molester, claiming that she'd had the babies in the toilet of her bathroom at home. She never told anyone who had done this to her; she had just mentally snapped and couldn't seem to face reality.

Another member of the group, Lorena, became agitated and yelled out, "Stop this foolishness, Maxine!"

Mrs. Bac said, "Lorena, do you hear me? Do not interrupt me or Maxine during discussion. Have respect for your group members. I will not tolerate this impolite behavior. The next outburst, you will be confined to your room."

Then Lorena looked directly at me and said, "What, new girl? No Miss Thang over there, not snickering under her breath."

I could not understand why Lorena attacking me. I tried to bridle my tongue, but this insane bitch had it coming, and my response was, "What? Oh, I forgot you speak Ebonics. No formal understanding of the English language."

Then Lorena said, "What, you think you better than all of us?"

I just shook my head at the nerve of this girl trying to challenge me. I replied, "Don't ask a question that you already know the answer to." Oh, Lorena was really acting out, raising up off her seat. The group members became quiet; you could hear a pin drop.

Then Lorena said, "What? Come again? Look, you just like the rest of us. You fucked up too, and don't you ever forget it, bitch. Walking around this place like you all that!"

I responded by saying, "Girl, sit down. You're becoming a spectacle; this is not a minstrel show."

Lorena said, "Sit down, bitch; don't let me get in that ass."

Then another group member, Carmen, said, "Sound like fighting words to me, Lorena. Ready to rumble?"

Mrs. Bac intervened by saying, "Calm down, girls."

Out of nowhere, I thought, "Let me get up off this chair and walk toward this girl." I looked her directly into the face. The next words out of my mouth were, "Listen, I'm only going to say this once. Step up or shut up. Oh, forgot you're hood. Let me say this to you in layman's terms. What's up? How do you want to do this? Do you want a piece of me? I'm begging you to throw the first punch; matter of fact, I'll do you one better."

I was about to throw a left hook when my roommate, Sonja, grabbed my hand and pulled me toward her chair. "It's not worth it, Mar."

Lorena said, "Yeah, listen to your girl."

I replied, "What?" Breaking loose from Sonja's hands, I walked over to Lorena, knocked her on the floor, jumped on top of her, and began to bang her head on the floor. I continued to punch her in that big mouth of hers.

Dr. Bac called the men in white, the orderlies, to pull me off Lorena. She was screaming at the top of her lungs, "You're crazy, bitch! You broke my nose, busted my lip."

Hearing Maxine in the background, I said, "I bet you won't interrupt nobody no more when they're talking." The entire group started to laugh.

Carmen shouted out, "Margaret, that's the homie! Got hands like a champ. TKO that bitch Lorena!"

Sonja screamed, "Jesus, oh Jesus, Lord, please save Lorena from the clutches of Margaret's hands!"

Dr. Bac told the orderlies to take me to the hole. Why would she do that? I was helping her as well. I said, "Why, Dr. Bac? Don't have them lock me up in the hole."

Dr. Bac said, "Margaret, you have to learn how to control your anger. You need to calm down. Spending a couple of days in the hole will help you sort out some of the anger that you have built up inside."

"A couple of days? You're going to have them lock me up? I'm not going. You're going to have to kill me. I do not know how you're going to get me there, because I'm not walking."

Dr. Bac said, "You will not talk with me in that tone, young lady. I will not tolerate such aggressive behavior from you."

I thought, "Why did this woman make me spit directly in her face?" Aloud, I said, "Fuck you, old washed-up cunt, manly ass bitch."

Dr. Bac said, "Gentlemen, take her away."

Margaret screamed out to the orderlies, "Do not fucking touch me! Put me down.

Dr. Bac, you can't break me, you can't break me, you can't break me, you can't break me."

Looking back at the group, I noticed that Sonja was crying as the orderlies took me off to the hole. Carmen was giving me the black-power fist; Maxine, her baby doll in her arms, rocked back and forth, waving good-bye. Then Dr. Bac said, "Now the rest of you, go to your rooms. Remember that if any one of you ever tries to pull the same stunt Margaret just made, you'll be placed in the hole."

I couldn't believe I was inside this dark, cold room. There was no light; I couldn't even tell if it was day or night. I was being treated as if I were an animal! Even animals were free to roam the earth. I had no one to talk with, and my meals looked like slop; they were not even edible.

The toilet didn't even work. The smells of urine and feces made me want to vomit. There was not even time for me to take a shower. The hole was somewhere I wouldn't want anyone to go—except for my father. The man who helped create me needed to be inside the hellhole that I was enduring. Isolation was exactly what Dr. Bac wanted me to feel. There was no bed, no faucet, no window—just me on this cold, concrete floor. This was for the serial killers, not someone like me.

After one week, I was still locked down. I had made a few friends in here: the ants that were climbing on the side of the wall and a little gray mouse that ran to one side of the wall, entering through a crack. A few roaches came out to greet me and then disappeared.

I contemplated suicide. Maybe if I put my head inside the toilet, the urine and feces would aspirate my lungs and suffocate me. Instantly, there would be no more Margaret.

By the second week, it hadn't gotten better. I started to have these crying spells that kept occurring; I felt totally depressed. Damn! I was having a harder time remembering how many days I'd been in this hole. I had no pencil, so I had to use my feces to tally the number of days on the wall. Feces stuck inside my nails.

By the third week, I basically had lost it. I had taken my feces and shaped little people. I wanted to talk with someone; why not my own poop?

By the fourth week, I was starting to see images of my momma. At one time, I thought I had died and was in heaven talking to my mom. I asked her to take me with her. She just smiled. I was becoming delirious and feeling like a junkie, even though I had never shot up heroin. I rocked back and forth, as if I were jonesing and the monkey was on my back. I was chasing my inner demon; I only saw the color of red flashes in front of my eyes. I ran along the side of the wall talking to my momma. I constantly pounded on the door, yelling for someone to let me out of this hellhole.

I even tried to proposition one of the guards and said I would give him fellatio if he would let me out. The guard laughed from outside the door.

By the fifth week, crawled up in a ball on the floor, I could hear the guards calling my name. "Margaret, your time is up. You have two minutes to shower, get dressed, and go see the doctor."

I replied, "What? Two minutes? Do you see all the poop that is in my hair, my nails, and my mouth? I want to look pretty for my momma."

The guard said, "You know she's in heaven."

I replied to the guard, "See, I've got to be looking my best when I'm going up yonder."

The guard said, "Margaret, Margaret, you're not in heaven; you're alive"

I said, "Oh, I didn't make it up yonder, but my momma just smiled at me. Why am I still here? I just want to go be with my momma."

The guard said, "You got an hour to get clean up. Then head directly to the doctor's office."

I headed to the restroom to bathe. I couldn't even stand up straight. Trying to gain my composure, I grabbed two washcloths, turned on the shower, and fell to the floor. I could feel the rawness of my reddened, bruised knees against the cold tiles. I cried profusely and nonstop, thinking that I had become tragic and that I was really turning into a basket case. Drying off from the shower, I looked directly at myself in the mirror as the steam cleared up. I was unrecognizable. There were dark circles around my eyes, and I had dreads in my hair; eventually, I would have to cut the ends to unravel them.

I just did not look like me; I didn't even know who I was anymore. Putting on a robe and slippers, I walked back to my room. I was thankful that Sonja was out of the room enjoying her recreation time. I had a minute to just relax. I grabbed the underwire-free bra from the dresser drawer, slipped on cotton underwear, put on a gray sweat suit, and brushed the few strands of my hair into a bun. I walked down the hallway to Dr. Dunbar office. I signed the roster and waited for the secretary, Mrs. Suzie to walk into the room. After Mrs. Suzie escorted me inside the office, I sat down on the recliner chair and was ready for the quack to start his assessment.

Dr. Dunbar said, "Hello, Margaret. Have you learned anything since you've been locked down?"

I said, "Learn what? You act as if I've been enjoying leisure time at a spa resort for the past four weeks. And I'm supposed to be the basket case!"

Dr. Dunbar said, "Margaret, watch yourself."

I replied, "Doc, you know what? Just because you're wearing that white jacket with a few letters next to your name, don't for one second think this insane asylum broke me. I've already been broken. Why you look so vague, man? What's wrong? The truth about me shouldn't hurt or get to you. You should be thanking God that you never had to experience not just what I went through but any of the things these young girls in here have endured. We all have been treated awful, but hey, it's my life, not yours."

Dr. Dunbar said, "Well, Margaret, what have you learned from the incident that has happened in the group while you were in the hole?"

I said, "You heard nothing that was said. You're just following protocol. I learned not a thing. Well, let me rephrase that; I learned that if you stand up for yourself in this place, you end up in the hole."

Dr. Dunbar said, "What makes you hit someone and then spit in your counselor's face? You have a lot of anger built up inside you, and you need to release all this negative energy within."

I asked, "Is that all, Doc?"

Dr. Dunbar said, "Well, we can talk later; you need some relaxation and much-needed rest."

Before leaving his office, I turned back and said, "Doc, I did learn something. Now I know what it felt like when my ancestors from Africa were taken and placed on those slave ships on top of one another and had to breathe in urine and feces. So, yes, I learned that slavery still exists. Bye, Doc!"

Dr. Dunbar said, "Wait, Margaret; before you leave, do you know the meaning of posttraumatic stress? Most prevalent ongoing effect of sexual abuse, a child who is traumatized by an experience of anxiety, powerlessness, terror, and physical pain. Often, children fear for their lives and the lives of others. The parent, the suspected wrongdoer, is more dominant than the child and uses his or her authority to achieve sexual abusive acts. This physical control can cause psychological effects; which includes memories, visions, hypervigilance, and separation from others."

I said, "You have a nice way of saying 'suspected wrongdoer.' He is and will forever remain my perpetrator. Good day, Dr. Dunbar."

CHAPTER 5

I walked to my room, and Sonja appeared out of nowhere. "Good day, Margaret!"

"Hi, Sonja!"

"Do you have time today, Margaret, to join me in prayer?"

"Sonja, can we do it another day?"

"Margaret, what if you never see tomorrow?"

I replied, "Sonja, let's pray."

Sonja said, "Margaret, kneel beside me. Lord, we ask forgiveness for our sins. Keep us safe from harm's way; send a host of angels to protect our souls."

That night, I slept in peace for the very first time since the passing of my mother.

Sundays were visiting days; no one had visited me since I'd entered this place. There was a loud knock on the door; it was Carmen wanting to borrow a ponytail holder. As usual, she was dressed like a boy. Of course, Sonja gave her a judgmental stare; she quoted the Bible.

Carmen said, "I'm a dike, butch, lesbo; you don't want to be my friend. Let me know."

Sonja said, "You're not filth; you're a child of God. The punishment for that sin is to be cast into the pit of hell."

I said, "Damn it! The both of you need to get dressed, no matter what. God created all of us in his image. We're created different for a reason. We should practice God's teachings and ask for healing and forgiveness through prayer."

Sonja said, "Are my ears hearing correctly?"

Carmen said, "Mar, you surprise me daily; I should never underestimate you."

"All right," I said, "let's stop this lovey-dovey mess and go to the recreation room; you two have a visit."

Sonja asked, "How do I look?"

Carmen said, "I'll smash. Come here, girl; give me the kitty-cat tongue curving to the right and left."

Sonja said, "You're vulgar. Do not, or I will never be into girls."

Carmen replied, "Don't be sleeping on us girls; we love getting you stray cats and getting you fixed."

I started to laugh hysterically. "Come on, Sonja, Carmen; let's go to the recreation room." I walked over to the magazine rack, and Sonja walked over to the table to meet with her grandmother; Carmen walked over to the table to meet with the social worker.

I felt that something wasn't right with Carmen from the grim look on her face. Carmen was sitting down, with her right hand inside of her sweatpants, legs crossed. Suddenly, the room became quiet, and all I could hear was Carmen yelling at the top of her lungs, "What, you think I'm' a shed a fucking tear over that bitch?"

The social worker said, "Carmen, your mom!"

Carmen replied, "I'm done with this bullshit; fuck that bitch. She fucking let muthafuckas pass me around like a fucking rag doll. See, it's all gravy, Mrs. Keller; you're my social worker, and you work for the betterment of me. Regardless, I can give two fucks if that bitch is on her deathbed."

Then, my eyes shifted toward Sonja, who was holding her grandmother's hands, begging her for forgiveness. Her grandma said, "Child, stop making a scene. Now, the elders at the church have asked that you confess to lying about the good ole pastor, and then you'll receive forgiveness."

Sonja said, "You're asking me to lie. Grandma, don't you believe me? I'm not lying!"

Her grandma pushed Sonja's hands away, stood up, and shouted, "Cut it out! Stop this foolishness! You're of the devil, spreading such filth in the congregation. I will not return until you write that letter admitting the truth."

Suddenly, as I continued to watch both Carmen and Sonja having one outburst after another, I felt something vaporizing inside my brain. I felt my soul leaving my body. It was as if everything from my past was drifting away slowly in a trance. I started to see red; it was blood filling my eyelids. I could hear the beeping sound; it had become louder. It was the voice of my aunt Silva screaming for help. I felt myself levitating and wondered whether this was what dying was like. As my soul headed toward a beautiful bright light, I could see the doctors and nurses beneath me scrambling for the paddles, trying to stabilize me. I was still unconscious, as I lay lifeless on the hospital bed. They were intubating and sedating me and hooking me up to more IV fluids.

All I could say within myself was, "It's not okay, Aunt Silva. I'm becoming caustic, and my soul is on fire; whatever you do, Aunt Silva, fight for my life because I'm becoming lifeless."

To Be Continued
Next novel: *Caustic the Avenge*

CAUSTIC

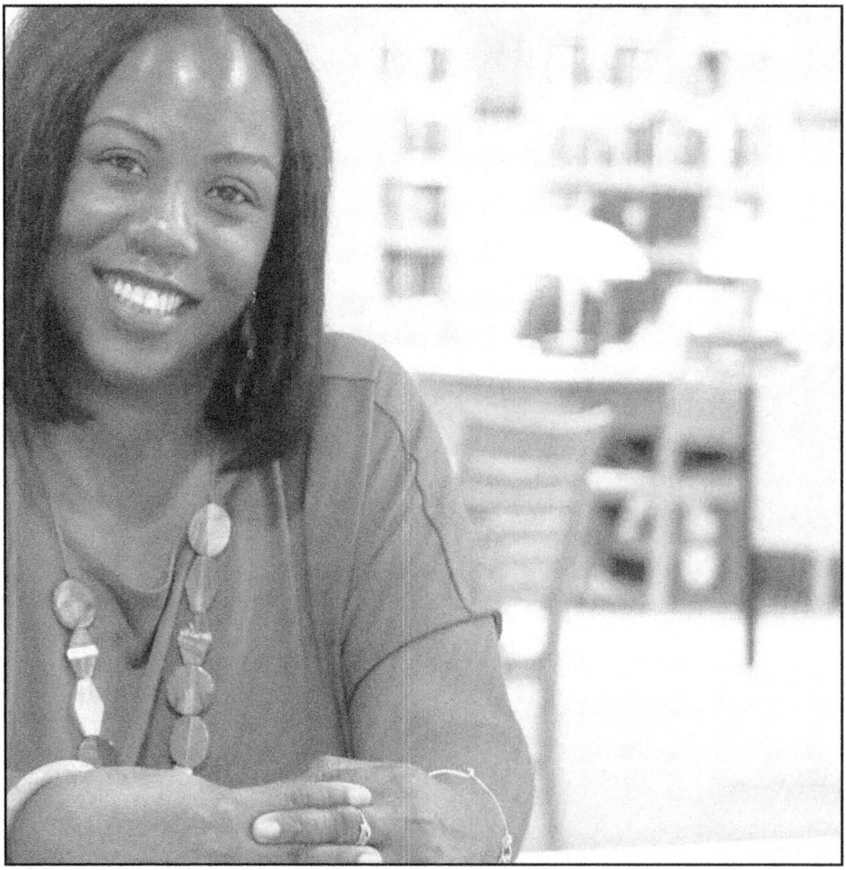

ABOUT THE AUTHOR

Tamesha S. Edwards was born in Berkeley, California, and grew up in the nearby city of Oakland.

Ever since she was young, Edwards has loved to read. She began volunteering in the library at her elementary school and was inspired by her mother to start writing in a diary. By the time she was in sixth grade, Edwards had written a poem, a play, and three books for her classroom.

Edwards continued to explore her creative side in middle school and high school. She later attended Merritt Jr. College and Cal State Hayward University.

Made in the USA
Coppell, TX
10 August 2024